THE

HIBOULEANS

A Novella Saga

Volume 1: BAD DAY

By

Octavia Reese

10 9 8 7 6 5 4 3

Electronic version, May 2014
Paperback version, December 2017
Paperback with revisions, June 2018

Cover artwork by Octavia Reese
Alcohol Ink on Yupo Paper © 2014

Cover editing and design by Joshua Jadon © 2017
www.joshuajadon.com

The Hibouleans logo design & illustration
by Octavia Reese © 2017

Illustrations by Jamal Lawson © 2017

Author's headshot by Misty Winter © 2017
www.mistywinter.com

ISBN 978-0-9995716-0-6 The Hibouleans: Bad Day

For Steven, Michael, and Ryan...

...and Tookie, my inner child.

ACKNOWLEDGEMENTS

Hi. Wow. Preparing this epic adventure for print is beyond my wildest dream. No – it is my wildest dream. My wildest dream, *come true*. Thank you to everyone that was an original supporter: Heather, Grace, Renee, Anne, Rachel (K), Dharma. When I never actually asked anyone directly to edit, buy and read my work, you did. I am so grateful to you for seeing me then and still cheering me on now. Thanks, too to my mom, that, despite not ever …*getting* me, did something right raising me, because I think I'm a pretty fantastic adult. No matter what, you've always reminded me I'm never alone, especially in the trenches. My launch team of saints – Nancy, Hillary, Oyatoki, Grace, Keena, Allison, Jenny, Ally, Austyn, Rachel (S), you pulled me through this. Whether you know it or not, your support to walk alongside me in realizing the first part of my biggest fantasy, is everything. I couldn't have figured out my typos, covers, business cards or headshots without you. To my Red Tent crew for holding me up and giving me reality checks when I needed them most. Joshua and Jamal for swooping in at the end and visually saving the day with your artistic prowess. Even my other-work colleague, Molly, is part of this team, whether you know it or not – because the organization I learned working with you has helped me stay on task as an independent author (outside of regular business hours, of course). My original child-readers, Asha and Steven. This is *for you*. And Jazelle – for helping me to be FULLY ME, and step into my role as the center of my life. And woven through all of this and all of you, God. Because God. The vision, the joy, and the love. It is all of God.

With warm gratitude,

Octavia

AUTHOR'S NOTE

I remember the first time the Hibouleans came to me… I was a newbie to authoring. My writing experience was drenched with high school and college literary analyses and sprinkled with personal reflections from seminars. I met actual writing in 10th grade at the unforgiving correction of Mercy High School's Mr. Mike Gruber. He always read the good papers aloud. I could never seem to make his Good List, but one day, I made the cut. My jaw dropped when I recognized my writer's fingerprint in the familiar word-flow. I started his class with Cs and finally learned how to write – as I speak. And then later, at the nod of the gleamingly amazing Dr. Stephen "Doc" Hemenway, my academic-Englishgodfather-figure at Hope College, I realized I was actually a *good* writer.

I was on an imposing deadline to hurry up and use my Miss America scholarships, which I had already deferred once when I became pregnant with Steven. I aimlessly joined the Masters of Art in Journalism program at Columbia College Chicago, but seemingly endless days monitoring Mayor Daley and City Council were wearing me down. I hated politics. With a burning passion. And while I learned invaluable skills: the power of short sentences, the glory of interesting verbs and the repulsing horror of the passive voice, my criticism remained the same, "Octavia, this isn't bad, but it sounds like a press release."

Of course! Why strive for something new when my natural tendency is to write releases? Well, I learned my lesson and eventually got published – twice – but I was already onto my next thing: PR. I dropped out of Columbia College and quickly became the go-to writer/editor of press releases for my account teams at Golin. It was glorious. But the corporate schedule at the time was unforgiving for a new mom and the cost of daycare pummeled by meager salary. It seemed pointless. My mind began to wander. Again. What could my next adventure be?

Enter positive pregnancy test number two. I had been studying mommy blogs for some of my PR accounts and figured, *hey, I'm a better writer than these ladies! And I'm funnier! I can do THIS. And get PAID!* I left PR. I was now a full time stay at home mom. I was good at it.

But blogs were…boring. I was soon the proud mother of one and almost-a-half children, but the neglectful parent of some soon-to-be-fully-abandoned blogs. And I was miserable.

I was one of the first of my friends to be married and have children. I crashed during naptime while they were packing for thrilling bucket-list vacations. I was up at night with a child eating from my breast while they were drinking and dancing with lactating-virgin breasts. I was a homeowner in a faraway burb of the burbs and they were all city-dwelling eligible bachelorettes. I was exhausted. I was unfulfilled. I was broke. I was isolated. I was lonely.

Still, I found joy in using my words to entertain. Since I was low on real friends, I imagined my own (something I now realize I've always done; in 5th grade, a very defining and excruciating year for me, I spent my days making origami animals and tuning out Miss Dawson, who seemed to resent me anyway. It wasn't my fault we were studying the exact same topics I had already learned in fourth grade at my previous school. I nearly failed every class out of disregard, but at least I had my paper friends.).

I wrote several short children's books that I was simply saving for myself. They were fun. Cute. Tiny adventures in youth. Some fingering the line between making children giggle and scaring them into behaving like angels; others, tugging at parents' aging hearts, aching for a time when others handled the tough adult stuff and our human suit were smaller, younger, more energetic. I loved these little stories. I always have. Chris

Van Allsburg was my inspiration. I wanted to be the Black female version of him, paired with Roald Dahl and garnished with a hint of Tim Burton and dash of Ed Gorey. But why was it that my favorite authors, illustrators, stories, characters, movies, and series, never looked like me? Why did white men get to have all the fun? My characters, my friends, looked like me and kept me company. They lived lives I could quite literally only imagine.

Michael was now fresh out the oven. I still wore maternity pants. What? They were broken-in and deliciously non-constricting. It was winter. January, I think. A thick blanket – several blankets, in fact – of snow coated our house, driveway and backyard, seamlessly blending it into the expanse of field just beyond the split-rail fence. It was stunningly pristine. I went outside, for what, I don't remember, because what happened next reshaped my life – *is* reshaping my life.

My eyes stopped on the strangest thing. There was a feather. And another feather. And another. I followed the trail with my eyes to a place in the middle of the whiteness. There was a pile of feathers, gently resting on the top of the snow as if those little hollow fluffy bones were gently kissing each snowflake on the cold white ground. There were no sounds. The air was still. There was no bird. There was no indentation in the snow where a body could have fallen. No footprints when it might have hopped weightlessly to its possible demise. It was like some giant bird had simply…vanished…in midair, in a puff of feathers. And so, the Hibouleans were born.

OCTAVIA REESE

TABLE OF CONTENTS

THE HIBOULEANS

PRØLØGUE

Taryn's lip trembled as she stared into Kale's eyes. Her chest swelled and recoiled with each deep breath. *In. Out.* The air entering and exiting her mouth were the only sounds in the otherwise silent cathedral. But in her ears, her heart became the execution drum, pounding a slow deadly rhythm.

Rage burned within her. She felt her eyes glowing in the shadows. But she hadn't lost control like she thought she would. Instead, she was poised. Beautifully strong. Steady. Her arm extended behind her, knuckles sore from her tight grasp, she was ready to spear Kale through the skull. She could smell his fear. And some part of her liked it.

Earlier that day, a passing squall had poured rain through the splintered roof. Plump droplets sizzled as they fell upon the stone floor, scorching after weeks baking under a relentless sun. And now, because of the night's coolness, the evaporating rain lingered in the humidity, creating a low fog that rolled over Kale's disfigured body and roiled in tandem with Taryn's breathing. As she watched, Kale seemed to shrink there on the floor. He was like a tiny child, swaddled in a churning mist.

"This is for your brother," she said, her words barely escaping her tear-packed throat. She imagined the sharp end of her metal rod entering Kale's head. She imagined throwing it with such force that it would pierce the marble beneath him, sticking into the stone with a dense clang.

But instead of launching, her arms withered to her sides; the foggy floor swallowing her spear with a muffled thud. Kale stared at the gray mist, where the weapon that could have taken his life fell, paralyzed with images of his almost-death. Taryn wanted to cry, but her tears lodged in her neck. She wanted to scream, but her voice was gone. A gentle hand on her back lanced her numbness.

"C'mon, Tare," Dayne said. "Let's go tell Parliament it's over." Taryn curled into Dayne's shoulder, finally crumbling into a sob. She cried for Ellen. She cried for Gram. She even cried for Kale.

While the owl is a solitary animal, a gathering of owls is

called a parliament

ChAPTER 1

Taryn strolled through the park. Towering elms formed an arc over the graveled walkway and the noon sun trickled through the boughs. It looked like it was raining diamonds. Taryn took a deep breath of fresh air and smiled to herself. She loved this park, its symmetry. The elms were perfectly planted in rows along the path; a mirror image on the other side. Every four trees, there was a park bench, and every four park benches was a kind-faced fellow park-lover feeding the birds.

As Taryn meandered down the trail, a warm breeze blew across her face and she closed her eyes to meditate on every sensation. Suddenly, a familiar face made Taryn's heart stop. Her mother sat on one of the park benches, reading a book with an old thick cover and feeding the birds. She looked up at her daughter and smiled gently. Taryn exhaled. Her eyes welled with tears. Feeling faint, she repositioned her feet to stabilize herself.

"Ma?" She could barely speak.

"Mommy?"

"Hi, my love," her mother hummed. She leaned forward on her seat, which was no longer a metal park bench but a large curving sofa with plush velour dark purple cushions; its wooden frame, painted white and trimmed with gold,

2

imitated the waves on the ocean. She tossed a handful of something from a bag to the odd-looking park birds, never looking away from Taryn's eyes. She gently put the book aside, still without breaking the locked gaze with her daughter. Taryn could hardly believe it. Her eyes and throat burned, and she couldn't keep a thought in her mind. She just wanted to absorb the image of her mother sitting in front of her. Alive. Talking. Smiling.

Taryn approached her, but stopped mid-stride, taken aback by the weird birds surrounding her mom. Fear flooded her body, erasing the warmth she previously felt. Some were walking with an eerie grace, and others just stood still, watching her.

They weren't robins or pigeons or sparrows, or any other bird typically found at a park. They were owls. Owls of all shapes, sizes and colors. A look of confusion swept over Taryn's face. Her mother, still staring at her, took another handful of the bird food and tossed it to the owls. Horrified, Taryn realized the feed was far from bird seed or bread crumbs; her mother was tossing handfuls of squirming insect-size mice, and the owls raced to pounce on their snacks.

"Don't worry dear, they like it," her mother said. Taryn began to think everything was an illusion and was about to run away as fast as she could from her imposter mother. But before she could escape, her mother stood up and smiled at Taryn once more. Taryn was frozen again. She didn't want to leave her mother. Even if it was a terrible nightmare, she didn't want it to end. Just one more moment. One more glimpse. One more smile.

Her mother lowered herself to her hands and knees and began to tug at the underside of the unique sofa.

"What are you doing?" Taryn pushed out, unable to hide the tears in her throat. She wasn't sure she wanted to hear the answer. Love, fear, sadness and confusion strangled her.

Her mother pulled her head from under the sofa and looked lovingly over her shoulder at her daughter.

"Helping you, of course. I love you so much." She smiled at her daughter, and the scene froze like a photo in Taryn's mind.

Taryn opened her eyes. She could almost see the chill in her room. She pulled a pen and journal out from under her pillow. In the dark, Taryn drew a hash mark next to the other twelve. This was the thirteenth time she had the same dream.

When Taryn rolled over, her heart stopped as her eyes landed on the glowing red numbers on her bedside clock. Also for the thirteenth time, it was 4:44am.

CHAPTER II

Taryn swatted her alarm clock. It wouldn't stop screeching. She picked it up and gave it a solid thud on the side. She groaned. The ancient piece of technology went silent. The old clock seemed so primitive, but she liked using things that had belonged to her mother. Taryn watched the red glowing numbers change from 7:05 to 7:06. Her eyes burned a little, hypersensitive to the sunlight spilling through her large bedroom windows. The inconvenient—and increasingly familiar—sensation was a symptom of Pellicularis. That's what Gram said, anyway.

Taryn groggily made her way to the wide mirror that sat on an antique dresser. She surveyed her tawny arms, speckled with marks. Taryn sighed. The hideous rash broke out over her whole body a few weeks ago. Even her face and hands were affected. At first, she assumed it was another humiliating symptom of adolescence, but no acne treatment made any visible difference. That's when Gram told her to stop trying.

"Pellicularis is when you develop your secondskin. You just have to wait it out, my owlet," Gram had said one afternoon.

Taryn questioned the origins of that pet name "owlet" Gram always used. But odd as it was, Taryn grew to depend on it. It felt like home.

"You should be excited," Gram had told her.

Excited was the last feeling on Taryn's mind. Not only was this phase mottling her skin, but Gram also said Taryn would start to notice a change in her vision and hearing as well. Gram couldn't predict how long it would last, and she didn't offer any remedies.

Taryn's eyes followed her blemished limbs up to her face and her heart skipped a beat as her eyes met their reflection.

Blinking several times, she leaned in closer to the mirror. For a moment, she thought her eyes had looked entirely black—as if her dilated pupils had taken over her entire eyeball. She shivered. The Pellicularis bumps prickled. She pulled down her lower lids and rolled her eyes around, revealing normal hazel Taryn eyes.

"I must be tired," she said to herself, blaming her nightmare-interrupted sleep pattern for her imagination overpowering her vision.

There was nothing in Taryn's reflection that soothed the discomfort of Pellicularis. Her wild brown curls were suspended around her head as if she were conducting an electric current. She sighed again. She didn't know which obstacle to tackle first. Perplexed by her own image, she tugged on the brass owl pendant around her neck. Another memento of her mother, Taryn never took it off.

"Good morning, my little owlet."

Gram's wispy graying strands of hair danced like feathers as she poked her sweetly smiling head into Taryn's room. Taryn relaxed for a minute and smiled. Gram's balmy voice was warm like a thick comforter on a cool autumn night. Taryn always found it musical, too—somewhere between the goosiness of a clarinet and the sparrowness of a flute. It was her piercing eyes that most people noticed first; intense but not convicting, and they always twinkled when she smiled.

"Morning, Gram."

Gram made a sympathetic pout, seeing Taryn standing hopelessly in front of the mirror. She came in and gave Taryn a tight squeeze.

11

"We're Hibouleans—no one like us in the world," Gram said. "And you, my owlet, are beautiful. I know it doesn't seem like it now, but this will pass, I promise. Pellicularis is temporary."

Taryn offered a weak smile. She didn't know any words that fit. Gram did enough talking for both of them, anyway. It was entertaining.

"Think of it as a rope. All those tiny threads woven together are impossible to break in one swipe. But with the right tool, you can cut through each strand, one at a time. So don't look at your woes all at once. Just deal with one at a time." Gram swiped an endearing finger across the tip of Taryn's nose.

Taryn nodded.

12

"Guard your heart," Gram said twirling out of the room and leaving Taryn to her own devices. "You can't trust everyone," Gram sang from the hall. "And sometimes, not even family. Breakfast's on the table.

Taryn thought that last part was strange, considering Gram was the only family Taryn had since her parents were killed. She knew she could trust Gram; she was an eccentric old lady and usually spoke in strange cadences—sometimes Taryn didn't know what she was really talking about. When she was younger, she used to ask for clarification, but Gram's explanations carried on for so long, Taryn eventually stopped asking. For the sake of her attention span, she learned to just smile and nod. Perhaps it was Gram's old age. Taryn smiled listening to Gram hum her way down the stairs and into the kitchen.

Taryn turned to the clothes she laid on a chair the night before. It was already scorching hot for mid-September and she would have to survive the day in a long-sleeved top and denim pants. Anything to protect herself from her classmates' judgmental eyes.

CHAPTER III

Taryn closed her eyes and inhaled deeply. Someone in her class wore baby-powder-scented deodorant. Someone else needed to borrow it. But she didn't have time to contemplate the bountiful odors of a high school classroom. Her lips unfurled a smug grin and with a sigh of confidence, Taryn strutted to the front of the class and began a presentation that would inspire Detroit Educational Club students for generations to come. Her own grandchildren would hear of her captivating presence, stunning wardrobe and impeccable elocution.

"Imagine sitting at the top of a giant pine tree…"

Taryn stretched her arms, illustrating the imaginary tree's unreachable height.

"And you sit perfectly still, like a statue, watching…and waiting…"

She had them. Her classmates perched on the edges of their seats, salivating for the rest of her story.

"Then, *SWOOP*…"

Taryn spread her arms out as wide as she could, pretending to soar in the air like a bird.

"…You bolt towards the ground, as if you are going to fly right through the Earth and come out in China on the other side…"

As she spoke with more energy and speed, smiles widened on her classmates' faces. She didn't just have *their* attention; now she had their *children's* attention. She was making history.

"And then, even though there is no evidence of life in the snow below, you stick out your talons, and in a half-a-second, you pull a mouse from its home underground and swallow it whole!"

Taryn had barely concluded her dance before the entire classroom of teens erupted in cheer as their friend, their champion, had them all convinced the owl is the greatest animal in the world.

17

Yes, Taryn thought, *their children's children will hear about this.*

"Owls are amazing be—becaw—" Taryn could feel a sneeze coming on. Her terrible allergies always had the worst timing.

"Ahh—ahh—"

She didn't want to. But she couldn't hold it in. Taryn sneezed with such force; it was as if her whole body exploded. Everyone in front of her was pointing and laughing. Looking down at herself, she realized why the joke was on her. When she sneezed, feathers had sprung through her skin, just like a piece of popcorn popping through its kernel shell. She would not be admired for generations to come; her not-yet-born great-grandchildren would never recover from the humiliation.

Another sneeze was coming. Her eyes watered. Her throat burned. The second sneeze hurled Taryn through the air. She spun like a trapeze artist. It was almost graceful. As she fell towards the classroom floor, her stomach told her she had reached terminal velocity, but her eyes told her she was descending in slow motion. Just before Taryn hit the ground, she whimpered, twitched, and threw her arms out to break her fall.

But she never hit the floor. One arm brushed her notebook and pen to the floor, while her other arm unconsciously assaulted her neighbor. Sandwiched between her auditorium chair and the fold-down desk, she was very safe from any public fall.

Taryn's ears tingled, and her heart crawled up into her throat as a wave of adrenaline rushed through her body. She blinked hard, trying to squeeze the fatigue out of her eyes.

Smirking, Dayne Graffen rubbed his arm where Taryn had elbowed him.

"Nice nap?"

Taryn had deliberately picked the middle of three empty seats to avoid everyone. The prospect of chatting for chatting's sake made Taryn nauseous and public speaking was an absolute nightmare. Literally. But even her wildest dreams couldn't have prepared her for this. The last thing she expected was to fall asleep in lecture and wake up touchably close to, as was widely accepted across campus, the most attractive boy under the age of eighteen. According to her memory, it was love at first sight. She was three and he was five. She was supposed to be sleeping, but her mother was entertaining some very loud guests. Taryn was going to see what all the excitement was about, but instead she found Dayne in the hallway, sitting on the floor drawing. Their eyes locked. He smiled. And she bolted back to her bed.

Eleven years later, not much had changed. Taryn opened her lips to respond, but no sound emerged from the desert that was once her mouth. Dayne knelt to the floor and retrieved Taryn's school supplies.

"Here," he said, placing them on her desk. Paralysis crept across her face.

"I was a little late today. Hope it's okay I sat here. The seat was empty, and you were takin' a snooze."

He flashed a brain-melting smile, further

rendering Taryn's body useless. Blood rushed to her head so fast, she had to grip her desk for stability. Beads of sweat broke through every pore in her body and the little hairs on the back of her neck stood on end. She considered running a finger around her collar to ventilate her turtleneck, but she couldn't convince her arms to move. She began to itch, worrying that Dayne was close enough to count her blemishes.

She cleared her throat, clenched her teeth and swallowed hard. Somehow, her neurons finally fired, and words fell out of her mouth.

"Thanks. I uh, I guess I fell asleep."

Dayne leaned closer Taryn as if to whisper in her ear.

"No big deal. Taryn, I've—"

She tensed at the invasion of personal space, even though part of her hoped he would cross the boundary even more. But their teacher shot a silencing look from across the small auditorium that cut him short. With her heart still lodged in her neck, Taryn was unsure how to survive the next ten minutes of this day.

ChAPTER IV

Dayne was a stunner. Almost all the girls from seventh to twelfth grade were dripping with crushes on him. But for Taryn, he was the last thought she had before bed and when she wasn't having unsettling nightmares about her mother, Dayne was the star of her dreams. He was sixteen, two years older than her, but age didn't separate classes in the mixed-grade lectures at DEC, short for Detroit Educational Club. At first, Taryn didn't know if landing a class with him was a stroke of luck or social homicide. However, being by all classifications nonexistent to most of the school body, Taryn often embraced her lack of social status, losing herself in her collection of fantasy adventure books. But three weeks into her fall quarter of classes, she was sure having her crush as a classmate was indeed the worst thing that could have happened – whether she claimed any high ranking social status or not. And there he was—close enough to brush just by extending her pinky. Of course, she didn't extend a single digit; she kept all her fingers flat on her desk and inched her arms closer to her body. She felt ridiculous.

Taryn scratched her arms and pulled her sleeves down to make sure the Pellicularis was covered. She pretended to fix her hair, shaking her frizzy bangs over her eyes, and peeked to each side of the room to see if anyone was watching her fidget. A timid glance towards Dayne temporarily relieved her anxiety—he had turned his focus to doodling in the pages of his notebook. Confident all attention was elsewhere, Taryn nervously toyed with the owl pendant, its eyes shiny from where Taryn's fingertips had worn through its finish. Thinking of her mom usually helped calm her nerves.

"...so, some guilty—or bribed—researchers leaked what kinds of organisms were really being produced: not just genetically-enhanced super cells, but genetically-enhanced super *humans*; supposedly for the rapid evolution of the Homo sapiens' immune system. There was some kind of huge revolutionary upheaval and most of the subjects escaped..."

Their teacher didn't just talk with his hands. He talked with his whole body and his enthusiasm was entertaining. He wildly recanted the centuries-old history of Detroit with such passionate charades that someone might think it was a first-hand account, not to mention the very first time the tale had been told. He was like a very excited and talkative toddler. But Taryn had heard the stories about the National Detroit Science Project hundreds of times. She already knew about the beasts that roamed the Bukes; everyone did. That's why there were giant spotlights surrounding the Residential Sector—the *Rez*, as everyone called it. The Rez didn't need fences to keep people inside because no one wanted to leave. No one wanted to risk being eaten alive.

"...The creatures headed straight for the Bukes and were never seen again..."

A holographic map of the city illuminated the white resin board at the front of the auditorium.

"Here are the walls..."

He traced the area with a laser pointer from his interactive glove.

"...And here's us."

With a little swirl of his red dot, he illustrated the twenty square blocks that made up the Rez. Between the Rez and the walls, there was nothing. The blankness on the map indicated the overgrown remains of a forgotten city—The Bukes. Whether the wasteland was named for being somewhat bucolic or because it was so fiercely rebuked for being inhabitable was debatable. Regardless of its etymology, the Bukes was the place to avoid. With another motion of his controller-glove, the teacher zoomed-in to the U-shaped building that housed DEC. He then rotated the map from aerial to treetop point of view, initiating a rapid bird-in-hyper-flight scan of the Bukes that abruptly ended at the miles-high city wall.

"Whatever happens out there stays there, between the walls and the Rez...could I have a volunteer please?"

Taryn silently prayed someone would volunteer. No one did.

"How about Taryn Massey?"

Even though she had that nagging feeling he'd call on her, she jolted in her seat. A few of her classmates snickered. She could feel Dayne smiling at her.

"No, thanks," Taryn mumbled dryly from under her bangs.

"I'll go, Mr. Ferguson," a chipper voice offered before anyone could object to Taryn's objection.

"Please, Kira. Please call me Ellen. I'm not old enough to be a 'mister.'"

Ellen Ferguson was more than just a teacher—he was the cool young visiting lecturer that insisted students call him by his first name. As far as looks were concerned, he wasn't a male pinup, but his charisma and the flicker of mischief behind his eyes made up for what his physique lacked. Taryn wasn't impressed.

Kira Farnsworth smiled.

"OK, *Ellen*."

She flitted her way down the aisle, her orange-ish curls bouncing on her back. Ellen quizzed her on the city's network of channels and rivers, and on the city's original industry. She passed with cute, squeaky, flying colors.

"Thank you, Kira," Ellen said. Kira bounced back to her seat, which was right in front of Dayne's. Her two best friends, who could have easily been mistaken for a hired entourage, grinned and congratulated Kira on her vast knowledge of history.

Taryn watched Dayne bend around his desk. Close enough to smell Kira's hair, he whispered a "nice job" in her ear. Taryn felt her face flush again, feeling a strange sense of betrayal.

"Taryn, you owe me a report tomorrow…" Ellen said, glaring at her. Ever since Ellen started at DEC a few weeks ago, Taryn felt like he was a little more interested in her than she preferred. He always seemed to be observing her. She hated the way he would stare at her during lecture. It was as if she was the only student in the room and he was speaking directly to her. Sometimes Taryn couldn't even concentrate on what he was saying. It was like words were coming out of his mouth, but his eyes were saying something else that only she could hear. He gave her the willies. And now, with his threat of a presentation, her one isolated bad day was about to become a bad day *streak*. Knowing Dayne would be part of her audience was nearly unbearable. The thought of embarrassing herself in front of the one person she wanted to impress the most was enough to make her want to fake being sick in the morning.

The bell rang.

Students rose from their chairs like a flock of geese ascending to migrate south for the winter.

"See ya," Dayne said, already out of his seat. Taryn tried to watch him exit but lost him in the gaggle.

"Okay everyone, have a great afternoon. Taryn… *tomorrow*," Ellen threatened. Now she really felt like she was in a sauna. A twinge of concentrated

horror sent her blood pressure through the roof for the
third time in an hour: tomorrow's spotlight would be on
her skin.

ChAPTER V

Taryn waited until the other students had emptied the room. Even though she kept a safe distance away from popularity, Taryn separated herself even farther from her peers once the Pellicularis debuted. But she normally enjoyed DEC. Since the Rez supported only a few thousand people, mostly scientists and their families, the school system had been modified to train the next generation of researchers. Instead of general subjects like English and History, DEC offered specialized intensive lectures like Ellen's "Evolving your Epigenome: The

History of Detroit" and Taryn's favorite, "The Bulls of Bashan: Brainless Beasts or Bankruptcy Bonuses?" Taryn often fantasized about being the first microbiologist-anthropologist to map and study the Bukes and its elusive inhabitants. Distracted with her thoughts, a bump from the side nearly knocked her off her chair.

"Hey, Tarry, wanna head to the lounge?"

Taryn exhaled heavily with a nervous chuckle. It was her best friend with a bad idea. Of course, she didn't want to go to the lounge. The lounge would be the best place for Taryn to bury her face in widespread humiliation.

"Pree," Taryn exhaled. "You scared me. I thought I was the last one out."

Priya Advani was born to be Taryn's best friend. If they weren't studying genetics, or acting out scenes from their favorite stories, they were taking martial arts lessons from Priya's three older brothers. At least they did before the youngest of the three went away to college. Lately the girls were the only members of their own book club, which they usually spent talking less about books and more about how they'd ever find romance in a place like Detroit.

If anything drew the girls together it was this: within the boring walls of isolation, they made up their own clandestine assignments, dreamed up scientific conspiracies, imagined being masters of self-defense...and sometimes, when they were the most desperate for entertainment, toyed with their schoolmates.

"Check it out." Priya slid a peek of a dart-gun-type tube out of her jeans pocket before stashing it out of sight again. A glint of mischief danced in her eyes.

"Wanna freak some people out?"

Taryn didn't stop her eyes from rolling in her head. But she also couldn't stop her lips from curling into a smile.

"Spitting rocks at peoples' heads is so gross."

"Yeah well, it's more fun than gross," Priya justified. "And people around here need to get shook up a little."

Taryn's eyebrows rose silently admitting the truth to Priya's point. She giggled remembering the last time she accompanied Priya on a pea stone sniper mission: the look of confusion on those monotonous drones' faces. The horror! The shock! It was better than television.

Everyone in their prison of a city was dreadfully boring and the two girls did everything they could to defy the norm. From countless adventures in thrill-seeking possibility to designing—and even beginning—construction on a bunker in case of a riot, the girls refused to succumb to the suffocating plague of mediocrity. They were the stars of their own blockbuster action film.

Priya was the yin to Taryn's yang; the practical to her analytical; the tactical to her systematic. There wasn't a plan Taryn designed that Priya couldn't execute. Priya was also the only one Taryn confided in about the skin issue.

"C'mon bumpy buns," Priya teased. The girls packed their books and headed for the door.

"Hey Taryn," Ellen said without smiling as they passed. His eyes were piercing, almost like Gram's.

"Hi," she mumbled, still trying to keep her head concealed. She choked down her unease and pretended not to care that Ellen would not leave her alone.

"For tomorrow, prepare to educate us on your favorite animal."

"Seriously? That's so…sixth grade."

Ellen glared so intensely the hairs on Taryn's neck lifted.

"Fine," he said. "Summarize gene replacement therapy as used in NDSP's epigenome project."

"Oooooh...." Priya's eyebrows nearly rose higher than her forehead as she failed to muffle a sympathetic reaction. She backed away from her friend as if the sentence were contagious.

Taryn sulked. She didn't know what was happening to her. She wasn't normally snarky, but there was just something about Ellen that made her bolder than normal.

"Um, favorite animal sounds great, Ellen."

"I thought so."

A delayed connection suddenly arrived with full force, spiking Taryn's heart rate once again.

Favorite animal? That's impossible, she thought as she remembered her dream. She only hoped real life treated her better than her subconscious.

"Well? Lounge?" Priya interrupted, pulling Taryn away from the teacher.

"Eh, not today…" Taryn said, more defeated than tired.

"Oh, c'mon… I bet *Dayne* will be there…"

Taryn quickly hushed Priya, glancing back to see if Ellen was within earshot. Dayne was the last person Taryn wanted to see—besides Ellen, but that was for a different reason. And Taryn, with her shyness, wild hair, and of all things, Pellicularis, was sure she wouldn't stand a chance competing for Dayne's affections.

"That's exactly why I don't want to go. You know he came late to class and sat next to me? I mean, *right* next to me."

Priya produced the most exaggerated face of excitement Taryn had ever seen. It made her nervous.

"Oh—migosh," Priya began. She had a habit of stringing several sentences together in one breath and Taryn could tell this was going to be a long one.

"…do you know what this means? He's so totally into you. First, you have to go to the lounge. That's absolutely mandatory because you have to follow up with him sitting next to you today. He was totally trying to connect with you. Then you need to find him, maybe bring him something, like, I dunno, candy, then you need to sit real close to him and accidentally rub his arm. You know like, 'oooh Dayne, you have a loose string on your shirt'…"

Priya's concept of acceptable behavior was slightly different from Taryn's own; she felt quiet observation was more valuable than talking just to be heard. Hunting down her crush simply to stand near him was the first thing on her list of *Things I Will Never Do*. But outgoing people are more likely to do things like that without thinking twice.

Sometimes Taryn wished she were more like Priya – facial features so striking that she could have been computer-animated, thick flowing black hair, deep brown eyes and flawless golden-oak skin. Taryn, on the other hand, was more of a frazzle-haired rashy high school disaster area. Her brownish hair never stayed where it was supposed to; her gray eyes seemed rather bland; and her skin, even under the disgusting pock marks, had always been a little blotchy.

"What if he notices...*ya know*? He'd be so grossed out."

Taryn shook her head just thinking about a scene involving both Dayne and her rash.

"Whatev," Priya gave up, slinging her bag over one shoulder. "The fearless move forward."

Taryn hated it when Priya said that: the fearless move forward. Taryn didn't like feeling that her shyness was a negative, or that being quiet was synonymous with being a coward. She wanted to reply with something smug like, *Yeah, but the fear*ful *stay alive.* But she didn't.

"See ya, bud."

"Sure, *dude*," Taryn muttered as Priya walked away, mocking her friend's boyish jargon.

"Bye Tarry," Ellen cooed.

Taryn groaned, wondering why *he* was still there. She started to ignore him but rationalized she shouldn't ignore her teacher. She had given him enough attitude for one day.

"Uh… see ya, Ellen…"

She wore a bad-taste-face as she spoke, looking more like she was sucking on a lemon than speaking to her instructor. She thought the words even tasted bad in her mouth just because she didn't care for the person she was speaking to. She prayed that would be the end of the conversation and he wouldn't say anything else.

But he did.

"Wait, Taryn… can I talk to you for a minute?"

Taryn could feel Ellen getting closer, which gave her chills and made the little bumps on her skin poke out even more. She grasped for an out, but Priya was already too far ahead to be reeled back in for moral support. It was like Ellen deliberately waited until Priya was out of range.

"I'm kind of in a hurry, Ellen…" Taryn whined without completely stopping her legs.

"Well, alright. I guess it can wait," he said, but quickly added in the same breath, "Just a Hiboulean thing."

Hiboulean? Taryn spun on her heels to reply, but Ellen was gone. Taryn tried to calculate how much time could have passed for Ellen to completely disappear. She walked back to the door, thinking he slipped back in the classroom. But the room was locked and from what she could see, empty. She couldn't shake the shock. Hiboulean. Taryn had only heard the word coming from Gram, and even she used it very little. Gram had told her she was Hiboulean—someone with origins in Hiboul. And only Hibouleans got Pellicularis. And that was that.

As Taryn walked home from DEC, her mind began to wander away from her teacher and the Hibouleans and back towards her delicious heartthrob. A smile grew across her lips as she imagined his pretty face. She dreamed about wrapping her arms around his neck and gazing into his gorgeous eyes. She imagined the big passionate kiss they would share and how he wouldn't want to let her go. Taryn felt the bumps of her Pellicularis prickle on her arms as her fantasy played out in her mind.

Groaning aloud with a smile, she swiveled 180 degrees. She giggled and vigorously shook her head as if to toss voices of doubt from her ears.

"I must be crazy," she whispered to herself, deciding to hurry back to the student lounge, meet up with Priya and hopefully catch a glimpse of Dayne.

As soon as the DEC lounge was in sight, Taryn felt sick again.

"This was a bad idea," she said aloud.

Ducking behind a cover of large bushes, Taryn weighed the consequences of following through with the lounge idea. Finally conceding to herself, she fluffed her hair, adjusted her clothes and then pulled her hood up over her face. With one last deep breath and a good luck wish, she stepped out from the bushes. And with a semi-confident strut, headed for the group of students.

CHAPTER VI

All of DEC must have filed into the only loitering-allowed area in the city. There were more kids than Taryn had anticipated, and it was going to be difficult to pick Priya out of the bunch.

But she found Dayne, engulfed by squeals, rather quickly.

Taryn blushed as her heart sank. As usual, a thick swarm of giggling girls surrounded him. Poor Dayne never seemed to have a moment alone. So attractive and popular, he was like DEC's own celebrity. Sometimes Taryn felt badly for him. Luckily, his three best friends, who were almost as attractive but much less gracious with their adoring fans, usually rescued him right on cue. Brandon Tell, Nora Samson, and Ronan Park arrived just as Taryn anticipated, cutting through the crowds and pulling Dayne off to safety. The girls whimpered like sad puppies. Taryn rolled her eyes. Although she was a little curious where he was headed and hoped to find some excuse to talk to him, she would rather be disengaged than be one of those squeaky groupies.

While Dayne disappeared in the masses, Taryn entered the cliques of mingling teens, craning her neck to spot Priya's thick black hair. But as the crowd enveloped her, she winced at the dissonance of dialogue. The noise stung her ears like smelling rubbing alcohol burns the nostrils. It was almost like she could pinpoint every word of every conversation simultaneously.

This must be what Gram was talking about, she mused. Her eyes watered from the auditory sensory overload.

"'Scuse me…" Taryn politely whispered, waiting for the seas to part. She remained unnoticed. Typical.

"Excuse me!" She called at the top of her lungs, triggering another throb of pain in her ears. No one seemed to even moderately sense her presence; she felt invisible as her requests went unheard. Abandoning her attempt at politesse, she embraced her inner bulldozer and began to push through the crowd. As she carved her path, one conversation caught her ear:

"Belle Isle is *so* creepy!"

"I know. Dare ya' to go out there past curfew."

"Heck no. And get devoured alive? You first…"

Distracted for a moment, Taryn paused to eavesdrop but became lost in her own thoughts about the deserted island in the middle of the Detroit River. The students realized she was listening and gave her an unwelcome glare. She sheepishly turned away from them, and continued in search of Priya.

"So, what are you wearing to Hunter's Fest?"

"I just downloaded this hot skirt and top for my OPP."

"Oo lemme see!"

Once again overhearing a passing conversation, Taryn listened to two girls gabbing about some party, another event taking place beyond her social reach. Taryn hung her head, certain it was a huge mistake coming to the lounge after all. As she navigated her way through the traffic jam of popular kids, the little self-esteem she had left became more and more diluted. Her strut dissolved into a sulk. Her presence was either ignored or rejected. Taryn felt excluded, and in the middle of the crowd of teens, she never felt more alone.

Taryn homed in on another conversation.

"There's no way you can bend three at once."

"Is that a challenge my friend?"

That was Priya.

"How much you wanna bet I can do it?"

Taryn recognized her friend's voice and her unmistakably competitive tone. Priya hated being doubted. If anyone told her she couldn't do something, she would nearly risk her life to prove them wrong. Sometimes her goofy personality and gift of gab reminded Taryn of Gram. Maybe that's why Taryn liked her so much.

"Bets, please! I'm taking bets! Two tokens apiece I can bend three spoons!"

Priya learned spoon bending from her dad who learned from his dad who learned from his dad in the hills of India. She said her dad could levitate twenty spoons at once and bend them in mid-air, all without using his hands. Taryn forgot about feeling lonely and laughed out loud as she watched her friend rake in stukas, a smash word for the student cash stipend the Rez gave to each minor. Their stipends usually ran out pretty fast since few teens know how to budget. But the smart ones, like Priya, had means of acquiring more.

Taryn pushed to the front of the circle that formed around her friend, who had climbed on top of a small coffee table. Priya spotted her and gave her a big goofy grin and wave.

"Hey, Tare! Think I can do it?"

Taryn held out two exaggerated thumbs-up.

"Pree-ya! Pree-ya! Pree-ya!" She began chanting for her friend. The others joined in, too. Maybe Taryn wasn't as invisible as she thought.

With all the tokens in a pile on the table, Priya asked for space and hushed the shouting. Even the distant conversations had ceased while everyone watched The Amazing Metal Bending Priya.

"Your friend is pretty confident, huh?"

Lost in the excitement, it took a minute for Taryn to realize someone was actually talking to *her*.

"What?" she asked, turning to find the voice's owner. Her stomach knotted in terror.

CHAPTER VII

From his 6-foot-tall height, Dayne leaned over to greet Taryn's eyes and flashed that familiar hypnotizing smile. He was overwhelming. For the second time that day, Taryn didn't know whether to laugh or cry. Her mouth felt dry although she was sure she was drooling. Her legs became putty and her heart fluttered like a butterfly in her chest. She thought about running away, but the tightly-packed swarm of students held her in place. Everything seemed to move in slow motion as Dayne's striking eyes twinkled. And twinkled. And twinkled. He was a vision of heaven glowing in the midst of chaos. Taryn was speechless.

"Your friend, Priya," he began again, "she's pretty sure she can do it."

Dayne's voice sounded like muffled music in Taryn's love-struck hypersensitized ears. She could hardly decipher his words into a language she recognized. Even if she knew what he had said, her mouth was paralyzed and incapable of forming a response. The best she could offer was an awkward chuckle of confirmation, which ended with a wet sputtering as she tried to eject strands of her mane that had wandered into her mouth.

The embarrassing attempt at speaking brought Taryn back to reality and she quickly flipped her head back around towards Priya. Taryn had become her hormones' punching bag and couldn't even label her emotions. She fought back tears and coaxed herself to breathe slowly. Shutting her eyes tightly and refusing to look at Dayne again, she tried to convince herself that she had imagined the entire episode.

Suddenly, someone cried from the horde, "She's doing it!"

Grateful no one was paying attention to her flirting fumble, Taryn rejoined the throng of Priya's onlookers. And there was Priya, like a statue; her eyes remained glued to the three utensils. She held the spoons by their handles in her outstretched fist. She didn't blink or move, and in her stillness, Taryn couldn't be sure Priya was even breathing.

A hush fell over the students and everyone gaped at the spoons. They began to bend away from each other. The set of silverware gradually unfolded like petals of a metal flower blooming in a time-lapse illustration. Priya remained motionless until she made the concave heads nearly touch her hand. When the spoon-flower had completely opened, Priya pulled her hand away, leaving the distorted sculpture hanging in midair. The crowd gasped. Priya smiled, still maintaining solid eye contact with her creation.

"Tah-dah!" She concluded, and let the spoons crash to the table.

The mob blew up in cheers and applause as the front row rushed the table to claim the bent metal as souvenirs. Priya jumped to a stance on the table, temporarily abandoning her normally humble demeanor, to bask in her own glory. Taryn laughed at the performance. She knew bending three spoons wasn't the height of Priya's talents. It was all a choreographed performance; the faked intense level of her concentration and her hard-earned victory were just proof of Priya's mischievous skills. Although she facetiously accepted the other students' praises, Priya really just loved to play with the easily-entertained high schoolers.

"Let's get outta here before they figure me out," Priya said laughing as she linked arms with Taryn. The two girls made a beeline for the street that would lead them home.

"So, Taryn," Priya jeered her friend with a side nudge, which unintentionally made Taryn miss a step.

"Dayne is so totally into you! He spotted you from like miles away and cut through the crowd to talk to you. Seriously, I watched him follow you! So, what'd he say?"

Taryn confessed her horrifying experience with some humor in her voice. She couldn't decide if she felt more shame or embarrassment, but either way, she chuckled in disbelief of how badly the scene played out.

"Pree, it couldn't have gone any worse."

Priya vigorously rubbed her friend's shoulder.

"Hey girl, no worries. Seriously. If you had seen the way Dayne stalked you today, you would be confident he'll be back for more. Even if you do get stupid as dirt around cute boys."

Taryn groaned. Pree was right, and although she hated to admit, she really was a blathering idiot around Dayne. A familiar metal-on-metal sound halted their conversation.

A safari-like train full of tourists slowed to a crawl with a low rumble. The side of the cars sported fancy lettering, *The Expo*, with streaks extending from the "o" as if the train was supposed to be known for speed. Below the flashy title was the proper name: The Grand Expedition of Detroit. After the city's bankruptcy and the building of the walls, the city council decided to try and reconnect with the outside world. The city gates open once a week for tourists to board The Expo, tour the city for a few hours, and try to catch glimpses of the escaped NDSP hybrids. One of the main draws was the Bulls of Bashan. Transforming performance-enhancing and injury-preventing genes was supposed to help professional athletes become athletic machines. But the cellular therapy instead resulted in giant beasts not unlike the mythical Minotaur. Although no one—Detroit residents or otherwise—had ever actually seen one, their story was frightening and therefore, an attractive headliner.

As an economic stimulus plan, it was a giant success. Tickets were pricey and every tour was booked for the next three years. The Expo would slow to a snail's pace at key observation points to let its passengers absorb their temporary and potentially dangerous surroundings.

Taryn wondered who put the Rez on that list of notable stops.

The Rez viewing station happened to be right in the girls' path. The train crept, and the passengers stared, clicking pictures of everything in sight, including the two Detroiters. The tourists didn't hide their degrading comments as if the girls didn't also speak English. To Taryn's sensitive hearing, it was like the visitors were whispering directly in her ears.

Look at them.

Zip my purse.

They look so…normal.

One of the passengers even tossed two coins at the girls. Apparently, they also looked like beggars to the tourists' foreign eyes. The girls put on their most threatening looks of disapproval.

"Snobs," Taryn cursed, loud enough to sound intimidating although she waited to say it until the last car passed them.

"I hate feeling like a caged animal," Priya said, turning her nose up towards the disappearing tourists. Then reasoning with herself as if to pacify her own angst, she added, "...but I guess it's the only way to keep funding NDSP's efforts to fix all their mistakes..."

The two coins that were so demeaningly thrown at them began to lift off the ground. They danced around each other in a helix and then swirled into a figure-eight pattern before landing in Priya's open palm.

"I wish I could do that," Taryn sighed.

Priya often explained that all matter, energy, and time are made from the same things, and if someone can understand how all the pieces work together, the potential of human ability is limitless.

Priya chuckled.

"I should have thrown them back in that guy's face. He probably would have died in his seat."

The girls stepped up to Priya's house. A warm breeze rustled the trees. Taryn closed her eyes to let the wind flow across her face. She was trying to wash the bad day away in the peace of the afternoon. But a tapping sound perforated the stillness.

"What was that?" she asked her friend.

"What."

"That squeaky creaking sound… it's so loud. You can't hear it?"

"No… Hey, wanna stay for dinner?"

Trying to shake the noise from her ears, Taryn looked up at the house, then its front garden, and the surrounding trees searching for the origins of the sound. Her eyes darted from ground to shrub to window to limb, but she could not pinpoint the noise.

Priya turned back to find Taryn on the sidewalk still examining the front yard.

"You coming?"

"Yeah, sorry…it's that noise…"

"So, I think I have an idea for how you can talk to Dayne…" Priya began. Taryn didn't want to think about Dayne or any other boy for at least a month. As Priya began to ramble about cute boys, Taryn's mind wandered elsewhere.

Around the back of the house, they climbed the stairs of a Turkish-style tiled porch and Priya, who finally stopped talking, unlocked the kitchen door.

"There!" Taryn whispered grabbing Pree's arm and pointing towards the back yard.

"Wha—"

"Shh!"

Taryn's eyes were fixed on the origin of the mysterious sound. At a corner of the sprawling backyard,

73

a tiny bird sat on a thin branch, bobbing up and down. The tree creaked from the bird's perch, and the tip of the branch made a squeaking sound as it rubbed on the second story window of the carriage house. Taryn's senses were on overdrive.

"Are you OK?" Priya studied her friend, who had vanished into some tunnel of thought where Priya couldn't follow.

"Hey," she said again. "How 'bout dinner?"

"Yeah, sure," Taryn said, returning to Priya's plane of existence.

"Just have to call Gram."

Priya's parents, the only physicians in the Rez, were still at work. Priya pulled out pakoras and mango lassi while Taryn headed to the communicator to contact her grandmother.

"Mella Delloguard Tannon," Taryn spoke into the com's microphone. Taryn and Gram shared the same middle name, which was also the name carved into stone above their house. Taryn never asked why they were named after the house. She thought it was a dumb name anyway.

"Hello?" The flat screen clicked on and the *connected* icon glowed. Taryn was surprised to see Gram sitting in shadows.

"Hey, Gram…why are the lights out?"

"Oh, I…just woke up from a nap…"

Taryn paused before responding. She couldn't help but notice something different in Gram's speech. But Taryn figured it was a derivative of Gram's just-woke-up voice.

"Alright, well I'm at Priya's and probably going to stay over."

Taryn was sure she heard a muffled kind of rustling in the background.

"What was that?"

"That's just fine Taryn. Stay there as long as you want. See you at home then bye bye."

Gram disconnected before Taryn could respond. Taryn furrowed her brow as she stared at the blank com screen.

"Hey. You OK?" Priya asked, seeing the confusion on Taryn's face. "You seem kinda funny today. I mean funny like weird. Like weirder than usual. For you."

Taryn paused a moment, feeling a nonspecific unease. Then it hit her like a ton of bricks.

"Gram called me Taryn."

"…and…" Priya asked with a full mouth. "…you changed your name in the last five seconds?"

"She never calls me Taryn."

ᑕᕼᗩᑭTᕮᖇ Vᒪᒪᒪ

"Dude. You're going to be late!"

Taryn groggily opened her eyes and Priya's goofy grin came into focus. She was already dressed and ready to walk out the door.

"C'mon owl chick. I've been trying to get your duff outta bed for like twenty minutes."

Taryn groaned. Priya? Owls? She hadn't told her about the nightmare with her mother, which happened again last night.

"You have to do your presentation, remember?"

Somehow, Priya had read her mind. Between her nightmare in the middle of the night and waking up now, Taryn had completely forgotten that she slept at Priya's and that she had a presentation to deliver in an hour. The previous night's events washed over her as she regained consciousness: after calling Gram, who oddly said her name instead of *owlet,* the friends giggled about boys and debated the NDSP hybrids' adaptations to survive the Bukes. Then Priya helped Taryn put together a few note cards on owls for her favorite animal assignment.

Hopping to her feet, Taryn tugged at her owl pendant, which was tangled around her neck. She threw on some clothes and tossed her belongings into her bag, while frantically whispering items from her mental checklist of things not to forget. Taking one last look around the room, she paused on her reflection in the mirror. Like catching the glimpse of an ugly Halloween mask, Taryn grimaced, shuddered, and figuring she didn't have enough time to fix the mess before her, bolted towards the door.

Still wiping sleep from her eyes, Taryn felt frumpy and disorganized when she reached her seat at DEC. She ran her tongue across her teeth, which felt like a row of fuzzy sweaters. She forgot to brush and imagined Gram singing, *"Haste makes waste, my little owlet."*

Raking a quick hand over her untamed hair, she retrieved a few feathers. Supposing they were rogue down from Priya's pillows, she dumped them to the floor. She felt like a shaken bottle of soda, ready to explode. Taryn hoped this was just another vivid nightmare from which she would awake in a few moments, but she knew her terrible morning was very real and probably about to get worse.

"Taryn, you ready?"

Ellen walked into the room ready for work. He hadn't even greeted that class before jumping into the day's assignments.

"You'll be great! Just remember what we worked on last night," Priya said, giving Taryn an encouraging nod.

Taryn reached into her bag for her note cards. Her heart rose in her throat then dropped down to her feet.

"Where are they?" Taryn mumbled through her furry teeth.

Hands trembling, she rummaged through her bag. She shot a desperate glance at Priya, mouthing, *I can't find my notes.* Priya returned a discouragingly nervous shrug.

Taryn could feel the bumps of her rash rise on her skin. They started to itch and she could feel the blood rushing to her face. Tears burned behind her eyes.

"This isn't happening…this isn't happening."

"Okay, Taryn. Come tell us about your favorite animal," Ellen boomed from the front of the auditorium.

Shutting her eyes tightly, Taryn took a deep breath and swallowed hard. Clutching the owl pendant around her neck for luck, she rose from her desk and hesitantly made her way to the front.

The room was dead silent, and her peers stared at her with blank expressions from their stadium seats. Priya, on the other hand, knowing Taryn had forgotten her notes, was no comfort at all and looked just as worried as her friend. Taryn searched the room for Dayne but couldn't spot his face among the teens. Slightly relieved that he wasn't there to watch her flounder, she tried to compose herself. Her hands became cold and clammy. She rubbed the owl pendant hanging from her neck to help calm her fears, but it wasn't helping. Her voice quivered.

"Um… I- I- I-uh…forgot my note cards, so I'm doing this from memory," she quietly stammered.

"Minus two, Taryn," Ellen said. He looked irritated.

"One for mumbling," he said from the back of the room, leaning forward in his chair and resting his forearms on his desk.

"...And one for beginning with an excuse. Continue."

Taryn closed her eyes, clutched her pendant, and tried to steady both her breathing and her thoughts.

"The...owl... is one of the—" She froze. The class stared at her, empathetically reflecting her petrified expression. Seeing her classmates glaring so pitifully at her made her brain shrivel.

"Okay, stop," Ellen said, moving away from his table.

"Take a deep breath and start over. This time, don't hold onto that owl around your neck…"

Taryn couldn't take much more of his critique. She was naturally a sensitive person, but being as vulnerable and nervous as she was on a second bad day in a row, she was about to lose it. She was particularly insulted by his comment about her necklace. He had no idea how important it was to her. She needed it.

"Everyone has a nervous habit, Taryn. Some people uncontrollably clear their throats; others fold their arms across the chest or keep their hands in their pockets. You know, I even saw a girl whisper 'ribbit' to herself over and over when she gave speeches."

85

A few kids snickered. Tears bulged at Taryn's eyelids, threatening to spill over the edge.

"That was a joke, 'ribbit.' You can 'ribbit' laugh 'ribbit, ribbit'," he teased. The class giggled. Taryn forced a smile.

"So, try again, Taryn. The words aren't important right now. You've done some research. *I hope.* Just tell me a story about owls," he soothed.

Closing her eyes and taking a long deep breath, she let her hands fall from the pendant and rest at her sides. Remembering her rehearsal from Priya's the night before, she started telling a story about owls.

"Imagine…" she began, sounding less timid. "…sitting at the top of a giant pine tree…"

Taryn recalled the words and confidence she had dreamed the day before. As if her subconscious had written and rehearsed the script, the words effortlessly flowed from her mouth. She gained assurance from her peers' faces and even Ellen, who seemed to be not only paying attention, but actually enjoying her performance. Feeling free and empowered, even her hands began to participate. They swelled with her words and stretched to illustrate her narrative. Her voice became stronger. She enunciated and projected.

Unfortunately, something, whether it was a cloud of dust she upset by her dramatic hand motions, or walking past a classmate that was marinating in an enormous amount of cheap perfume; something triggered a sneeze. Her dream. Taryn's subconscious had warned her. She couldn't catch her breath as her diaphragm pulled back her lungs like a taut archer's bow. Her eyes rolled back in her head. Her ears closed. Her mouth opened. Her hands rose towards her face. And in a split second, with her brow furrowed and her eyes shut, she released a sneeze that could have launched a rocket to the moon.

Body fluids left her face at an alarming rate, sending her backwards. Unable to catch herself from falling onto the floor, her t-shirt flew up around her chest revealing her speckled midriff. Mortified, she scrambled to cover her rash, wipe the snot and spit from her face, and somehow try to regain a centimeter of poise.

Ellen looked equally embarrassed and raced to her side to help pick her – and her modesty – up off the floor.

She sheepishly glanced to her classmates. Priya was on her feet looking concerned. The front row was taken aback, and looking disgusted at the spray of Taryn-spit that coated their desks. The rest of the room was consumed by laughter.

Taryn surveyed the young teens. They seemed to be mocking her in slow motion. She saw their guffaws, but in her dismay, they seemed to be as silent as mimes. Tears streamed down her face and she bolted up the auditorium aisle towards the door.

Taryn abandoned DEC for home, unable to consider staying for the rest of the day's lectures. She didn't know how to collect her thoughts or even begin to put the many pieces of her disappointment in order. She just wanted to go to sleep and wake up in ten years.

CHAPTER IX

Typical for mid-morning, the neighborhood streets were empty. Taryn sulked her way home free from passers-by or teen gawkers from class. Although she felt utterly hopeless, she tugged on her owl pendant, wishing her mother would be at home to hold and console her. Taryn paused for a moment and looked up towards the sky. She let the sun pour over her face, wet with tears.

One after another, defeating thoughts intertwined in Taryn's mind, entangling her in a net of pity she just couldn't escape. She found herself trying to sort through every little thing she wished she could change about herself. She wanted more confidence. She wanted to feel important. She wanted a more exciting life. Most importantly, she wanted the Pellicularis to be done. Suddenly Gram's metaphor about the rope made sense. As she reached the front steps of the sprawling Delloguard house, she decided to ask Gram what Hibouleans do to stop Pellicularis. Taryn pushed open the gigantic wooden door, and with a deep breath of readiness, she called her grandmother.

"Gram!"

Her voice echoed throughout the formal entryway of the old mansion. It was her grandmother's house, and, according to Gram, had been in the family for generations. Nearing 300 years old, the house contained decades of secrets. Taryn could feel them. Sometimes it felt like the house was alive.

"Gram?"

Taryn dropped her bag in the foyer and strolled into the giant stair hall. The almost limitless ceiling in the hall made the entry breathtaking to every first-time visitor. Even Taryn had to stop to admire it every now and then, even though she passed through it daily. The home was made with the type of passion that immortalized its creators' skills and talents for centuries.

Listening for a response, Taryn glanced across three doors: one leading into the kitchen, another leading to a long hallway, and the last opening to the first of two grand sitting rooms.

"Hey, Gram?"

Only the house responded with creaks and groans. It seemed to be breathing.

Gram was always there when Taryn got home from DEC. She never left the house except to go outside and garden. Since Taryn's parents died when she was a child, she had lived with her grandmother in the same house where her mother had grown up. Even though the house scared her sometimes, she took comfort in knowing that years ago, her own mother was also a teenage girl there, studying and sleeping in the same bedroom Taryn had now. Gram was all Taryn had. No parents. No siblings. No aunts or uncles. Everyone was a victim of an untimely death. An illness here, a freak accident there.

And now, for the first time in her life, Gram was not where Taryn expected her to be.

Beyond the stair hall, the first floor was a row of rooms; each room had three doors: one to each side leading to adjacent rooms, and one door on the back side of the house that led to a long hallway that was made of glass that framed the gardens like a beautiful painting. Gram had explained to Taryn that it was intended for servants, who could scurry around from room to room to wait on their employers without disturbing them or their company. She rushed through the rooms: the two sitting rooms, the library, and finally the solarium. She threw open the giant patio doors leading to the meticulously cultivated gardens.

"Gram?"

Still no response. Taryn returned to the stair hall. The thick slabs of marble that made the staircase wound around the gaping cylindrical hall, opening to a massive crystal chandelier delicately suspended in midair above the third floor. Aside from one giant greasy black feather at the base of the staircase, nothing was out of the ordinary. Taryn studied the feather for a moment, but decided not to touch it. It looked diseased, although she couldn't picture whatever massive animal created it.

She dashed up the cascading flight of steps hoping Gram was there. At the top, Taryn realized she had scaled the stairs at a nearly impossible pace. With little effort, she had taken four steps at a time, flying past grade school photos of her mother and uncles and aunts she never met. She barely saw her parents' wedding picture, which was a blur at her preternatural speed. Taryn released a quiet laugh of intrigue, crediting Pellicularis for her sudden surge in strength and energy.

Taryn faced the wide second-floor hall, scanning for signs of life or evidence of foul play. Suddenly, her Pellicularis bumps all prickled in unison and Taryn felt a charge of energy flow through her as her eyes landed on an array of feathers on the floor—just like the one from downstairs. There were thousands of them. They were like the remnants of an intense pillow fight—with really big pillows stuffed with really big feathers.

She kneeled down to observe them, but a bouncing light distracted her. Following the flicker, Taryn found a nearly invisible handle of a door made to look like the wall.

"The Corridor," she whispered, abandoning the feather-pile and approaching the passageway.

It might as well have been the first time she noticed the hidden wing of the house—it was never used, and Taryn had only a few memories, all of which were frightening, of its deserted halls. She tried the knob. It was unlocked. She breathed deeply, pushing aside any fears she was too nervous to call by name.

"The fearless move forward," she coached herself, thinking of Priya.

Taryn leaned into the heavy piece of wood, which was so thick, she felt more like she was trying to move the whole wall. Finally it gave, and the shadowy Corridor unfolded before her.

CHAPTER X

Inside, Taryn lingered in the dark hallway. Sunlight from the landing window glowed through the open door behind her, casting a long slender shadow on the oriental runner. A mirroring patch of natural light at the opposite end of the hall indicated the end of the tunnel. But between the two lit-areas, Taryn stood in the darkness. She counted slits of light along the floor, which implied the several doors she knew lined the hall. There should have been sconces on the wall, she remembered, and ran her hand along the ancient textured wallpaper.

98

She couldn't feel a switch, but her eyes seemed to be adjusting abnormally well to the darkness.

"Gram?"

Her voice didn't even echo. It was like she was screaming into a pillow. Taryn began to have second thoughts. Sure, it seemed like a great idea to look for Gram up in that creepy wing, but the farther away Taryn got from her port of entry, the more she felt like a first-time swimmer drifting out into the ocean with the security of the beach fading into the distance. The isolated wing was the one part of the house they never used. Ever. Taryn had only been in there a handful of times and knew nearly nothing about its purpose. Only one thing ever pulled her to venture through the secret door: the massive rendering at the end of the hall. It was a hand-drawn map of the old city. Taryn would trace its streets and highways with her eyes until her fear overtook her and she'd race back to the safe side of the house.

From above, the double-decker branch of the home gave Delloguard a T-shaped floor plan. Its ground level was a wall-less walkway that divided the back gardens in half. Towering pillars formed large swooping arcs, giving the stilted peninsula the feel of a French cloister.

About a hundred feet from where Taryn lingered on the second floor, a large stone staircase wound around itself, leading up to its third-level and pinnacle: a sprawling ballroom with balconies overlooking the gardens. As she reflected on the beautifully strange unused space, Taryn realized a crucial detail she had never noticed before—the wall-door behind her was the only entrance to the mysterious wing. There was no way up from the gardens and no way out from the ballroom. Taryn shuddered.

"Gram?" she called, a little more guarded.

She decided it was time to try one of the doors. Spying the first light slice to her right, she reached for the handle. Locked. She paused to read a small bronze plate affixed at eye-level. *Paradise*, it read. Across the hall was another. *Utopia*. Locked. The next three doors were also locked. *Nirvana. Bliss. Rapture.*

Focused, Taryn continued. She tugged on knobs and called for her grandmother. *Ecstasy. Joy.* But the Corridor of pleasure seemed to be swallowing her alive. Then, *click*. The next handle turned unexpectedly. *Oasis*.

Taryn's heart pounded as her hand rested steadily above the handle. She hadn't even turned the knob yet. She hesitated before pushing the heavy door inward. But when she did, the bright world on the other side took her breath away. The ceilings were so high that Taryn imagined the tallest tree she had ever seen could probably fit in there and still not touch the top. A fresco of the most stunning cloud-filled sky adorned the ceiling, and the morning light gave the illusion of sunset. The wall opposite the door was completely glass, with blue fabric draping down like water spilling over a cliff. Live vines crawled up the corners where the windows met the walls, and Taryn could count at least twenty sparrows darting between them, unaware in the nature-authentic décor that the real world was on the other side of the glass.

"Wow," she gasped aloud, enthralled by the beauty of the room.

She wandered about the room's perimeter, squatting for a moment to trace the elaborate pattern of the immaculate parquet floor. How could she not know this ethereal paradise was in her own home?

Across from the windows and balcony, a gold and marble kitchenette with an L-shaped eating bar triggered a pang of hunger in Taryn's stomach. The Oasis door separated the kitchen from towering rows of built-in shelves, which were filled with books of all shapes, sizes and colors. The wall facing the kitchenette housed a massive stone fireplace, with a huge mirror on the mantel. In the middle of the room, facing the fireplace was a striking seating arrangement around a Turkish rug.

Taryn walked towards the fireplace, peeking her head into the first of two doors, which led to a bedroom. The windowless room was just as immaculate as the main area, with unreachable ceilings and impressive décor. On the other side of the fireplace, the second opening led to a lavatory. Equally ornate, she admired a wall of shelves with glass doors that held linens and decorative toiletries. Taryn suspected another door inside the bathroom connected the adjacent bedroom.

When she turned to face the apartment again, her jaw dropped to the floor. Her Pellicularis prickled. An onlooker might suspect she had just caught a regretful glimpse of a monster or some other gigantic hideous insect.

"No way," she said to the sparrows. They seemed to acknowledge her, playing tag across the ceiling before finding new resting places. Her body was trembling with adrenaline as she recalled her disturbing recurring dream. That beautiful park and her mother feeding owls. The image of her mother sitting on that deep purple couch – and that couch was staring Taryn in the face, furnishing the strange apartment. Taryn remembered her mother's words.

"Helping you, of course," she had said. And before Taryn realized what she was doing, she was on the ground, sweeping the underside of the sofa with one hand.

OCTAVIA REESE

"Owlet"
Cover art by Octavia Reese
Alcohol Ink on Yupo Paper
© 2014

OCTAVIA REESE

Look for

THE
HIBOULEANS

A Novella Saga

Volume 2: LITHIUS

Summer 2018

Follow the author online

www.octaviareese.com
www.facebook.com/oabooks